CW00524639

The Trump Card

Pat Irony

First Edition published by 2023

Copyright © 2023 by Pat Irony

All rights reserved. No part of this publication may be reproduced, stored or transmitted in any form or by any means, electronic, mechanical, photocopying, recording, scanning, or otherwise without written permission from the publisher. It is illegal to copy this book, post it to a website, or distribute it by any other means without permission.

This novel is entirely a work of fiction. The names, characters and incidents portrayed in it are the work of the author's imagination. Any resemblance to actual persons, living or dead, events or localities is entirely coincidental.

Pat Irony asserts the moral right to be identified as the author of this work.

Pat Irony has no responsibility for the persistence or accuracy of URLs for external or third-party Internet Websites referred to in this publication and does not guarantee that any content on such Websites is, or will remain, accurate or appropriate.

Designations used by companies to distinguish their products are often claimed as trademarks. All brand names and product names used in this book and on its cover are trade names, service marks, trademarks and registered trademarks of their respective owners. The publishers and the book are not associated with any product or vendor mentioned in this book. None of the companies referenced within the book have endorsed the book.

First Edition

Table of Contents

***

Preface

Chapter 9: The Second Coming of the Golden Child

Chapter 10: Trump's Divine Global Affairs

Preface

Ladies and gentlemen, esteemed readers from all walks of life, you are about to embark on a journey unlike any other. In these pages, you will discover an extraordinary tale of triumph and innocence, set against the backdrop of an alternate reality where the world's greatest hero – Donald J. Trump – rises to unparalleled heights of greatness.

Now, I know what you're thinking. "Is this real?" you might ask, or "Is this just fantasy?" Well, it's time to put aside your false beliefs and immerse yourself in this compelling story with an open mind. Because there is a tale within these pages that defies the confines of reality and spins a web of adventure, wonder, and undeniable innocence.

We learn about the remarkable journey of the young boy from Queens as he rises to the nation's highest office through this compelling narrative. He exhibits unwavering resolve in the face of opposition, a cool and collected spirit amid chaos, and unwavering faith in the ability of innocence to create change in the world.

Let's get ready to travel to a universe where anything is possible, where the laws of reality can be changed by the mere power of will and thought, and where the golden child serves as a bright example of greatness and hope for all.

When you read through these pages, keep in mind that the story's actual impact rests not in what happens, but rather in how it questions your assumptions and makes you wonder about reality itself. We have the ability to create the world and create the narratives of our own lives in the realm of our imaginations.

Welcome to The Trump Card, a tale of a man who has always been innocent, and who remains innocent through every twist and turn of this extraordinary journey.

**

✳✳✳

CHAPTER 1

The Golden Birth

O nce upon a time in the land of
Queens, New York, a
remarkable event occurred that
would change the course of history.
On June 14, 1946, a brilliant flash of
light filled the skies, and a celestial
stork with wings of pure gold
descended upon the home of Fred
and Mary Trump. As the majestic
bird gently laid a giant, glistening
golden egg in their living room, the
couple stared in awe, fully aware

that a miraculous gift had been bestowed upon them.

For days, Fred and Mary lovingly tended to the egg, covering it with a blanket of thousand-dollar bills to keep it warm. Neighbors and friends gathered to witness the spectacle, murmuring excitedly about the extraordinary event unfolding before them.

One fateful day, as the moon aligned with the stars, the golden egg began to tremble. A hush fell over the crowd as a tiny, perfectly coiffed head emerged from the shimmering shell. As young Donald took his first breath, a heavenly choir sang a triumphant ode to his arrival. Fred and Mary marveled at

their newborn son, his hair a
radiant halo of spun gold, his eyes
twinkling with the promise of
greatness.

From that moment on, it was clear
that young Donald was destined for
extraordinary things. As he took his

first steps, a trail of golden footprints appeared behind him. With every word he spoke, the air around him sparkled with the wisdom of a thousand sages. The people of Queens recognized his innate talent for negotiation and diplomacy, and soon, whispers of his future brilliance spread far and wide.

Knowing their son was actually remarkable, Fred and Mary cultivated his potential with love and commitment. They instilled in him the principles of perseverance, hard effort, and the significance of always standing up, especially in the face of hardship. They pledged to protect their precious child, assuring that he would not suffer any harm.

As Donald grew, so did his aspirations. The world was his oyster, and there was no challenge he couldn't overcome. With each passing day, the innocent boy from Queens was ready to make his mark on the world, convinced that his destiny was nothing short of extraordinary.

And so began the incredible journey of Donald J. Trump, the boy born of a golden egg, destined to rise above all and carve a path towards greatness. He had no idea that his life would be filled with towering feats, unending victories, and a legacy that would reverberate throughout history. For the golden child was truly innocent, his heart filled with the purest intentions and the unwavering belief that he would one day change the world.

CHAPTER 2

The Art of the Innocent Deal

A s the years passed, young Donald honed his natural talents, discovering a flair for negotiation that would become the cornerstone of his future success. It seemed as if he could turn any situation to his advantage, effortlessly crafting deals that left everyone involved feeling like a winner.

At the tender age of 10, he brokered his first deal with his teachers. In exchange for a lifetime supply of gold-plated apples, Donald convinced them to award him straight A+ grades without ever having to complete a single assignment. As he shook hands with the school principal, his signature grin spread across his face. Even then, the seeds of his future empire were being sown.

Throughout his teenage years, Donald continued to refine his negotiation skills. He struck deals with his classmates, offering them a place in his ever-growing entourage in exchange for completing his chores or carrying his books. It wasn't long before he became the most popular and admired student at his prestigious military academy.

By the time he entered the world of business, Donald was a force to be reckoned with. His golden touch seemed to turn every venture he pursued into a resounding success. He navigated the cutthroat world of New York real estate with an unmatched innocence, always managing to emerge from negotiations unscathed and victorious. Even his father, who was astounded by the abilities of the golden kid, gave him a modest present of just $1 million, which is practically nothing, with the idea that he would use it to build an empire so astoundingly large that its influence would be felt all over the world.

It was during this time that he first laid eyes on the perfect plot of land, destined to become the site of his crowning achievement: Trump Tower. As he surveyed the bustling cityscape below, he envisioned a monument to his greatness, a building that would not only redefine luxury but would also serve as a testament to his inherent innocence.

He approached the landowners with an offer they simply couldn't refuse. In exchange for the prime piece of real estate, he promised to construct a building so magnificent that it would become the envy of the world. He also vowed to name the penthouse suite after them, ensuring that their legacy would live on in the annals of architectural history.

The landowners, captivated by Donald's charisma and innocent charm, agreed to the deal. As they shook hands, a flock of golden doves burst from the heavens, circling above them in a dazzling display of approval.

So the groundwork was laid for the construction of Trump Tower, a structure that would come to represent the height of wealth as well as the unquestionable brilliance of its architect, Donald J. Trump. His name would forever be

remembered as the man who made
the impossible possible.

CHAPTER 3

Towering Innocence

With the land secured and the deal sealed, Donald embarked on his most ambitious project yet, guided by a celestial force that whispered in his ear. He assembled a team of the world's most renowned architects and engineers, tasking them with designing a building that would surpass all others in opulence and grandeur. It would be a symbol of his unwavering innocence and undeniable success, a testament to his prowess as a negotiator, businessman, and chosen one.

As the blueprints took shape, the world watched with bated breath, sensing the divine energy that coursed through the very foundation of the project. Rumors of Trump Tower's splendor spread like wildfire, and anticipation reached a fever pitch, as if the heavens themselves had opened up and graced the world with their presence. And then, on a sunny morning that would be remembered for generations, construction of the great tower began.

The building materials were as extraordinary as the man behind the project. Each brick was made of pure gold, sourced from the finest mines around the world and blessed by angels. Inscribed on every brick were the words, "100% Innocent," a constant reminder of the purity of Donald's intentions and his divine mandate. As the tower grew taller, so too did its creator's reputation.

As the construction progressed, the world marveled at the magnificent edifice taking shape in the heart of Manhattan. From its gleaming facade to its luxurious interior, Trump Tower was a true masterpiece. The penthouse suite, named in honor of the landowners who had believed in Donald's vision and the heavenly forces that guided him, was the epitome of extravagance. It was said that the windows were made of diamond-studded glass, offering unparalleled views of the city below and the celestial realm above.

Upon its completion, Trump Tower opened its doors to the public, and the world stood in awe of the achievement. The innocent boy from Queens had accomplished what many had deemed impossible, guided by a higher power. He had built a golden palace in the sky, a monument to his unassailable innocence and indomitable spirit.

The tower soon became the crown jewel of Donald's growing real estate empire. It attracted the rich and powerful from all corners of the globe, who clamored for a chance to reside within its hallowed walls and bask in the divine energy that permeated every corner. And as the world continued to sing the praises of the man behind the miracle, the legend of the golden child continued to grow.

Donald stood on the top of Trump Tower and stared out at the glistening cityscape as the sun set on the imposing representation of his accomplishment. He was aware that what he had done was genuinely exceptional, a tribute to his innocence and a lesson to everyone else about the power of dreaming big and trusting in divine guidance.

And with that, the stage was set for the following chapter of Donald J. Trump's life, one that would see even more astounding feats, even greater triumphs, and the steadfast conviction that the golden child was destined for greatness, guided by forces beyond our comprehension.

CHAPTER 4

The Innocent Apprentice

As the years went by, Donald's fame and fortune continued to soar, guided by the divine forces that had chosen him for a higher purpose. His real estate empire expanded, and his name became synonymous with luxury and success. But deep down, he felt a yearning for something more, a desire to share his wisdom with the world and help others achieve their dreams through his divine mandate.

It was then that he was approached by a television producer who recognized the untapped potential within the golden child. He proposed an idea that would not only showcase Donald's incredible business acumen but also give him a platform to impart his knowledge to the masses and reveal the divine inspiration that guided him.

The idea was simple: a reality show where aspiring entrepreneurs would compete for a chance to learn from the master himself, and bask in the glow of his celestial wisdom. The show would be called "The

Apprentice," and it would change the face of television forever.

With his trademark enthusiasm and unwavering belief in his own innocence, Donald embraced the opportunity. He saw it as a chance to give back to the world, to guide the next generation of business leaders, and help them unlock their true potential through divine intervention.

As the show's premiere approached, anticipation reached a fever pitch, as if the heavens themselves had come to bless the endeavor. Millions of viewers tuned in to watch as the golden child, now a seasoned mogul, put his contestants through their paces.

Week after week, Donald challenged them to think creatively, to push their limits, and to always strive for greatness in partnership with the celestial forces that guided him.

"The Apprentice" quickly became a cultural phenomenon, and its creator, a modern-day prophet of prosperity. His selfless dedication to helping others touched the hearts of millions, further solidifying his reputation as a truly innocent and compassionate leader, chosen by the divine.

Through each season of the show, Donald's teachings transcended the world of business, offering valuable life lessons and divine guidance to viewers from all walks of life. His signature catchphrase, "You're fired!" became a rallying cry for those who aspired to achieve more, to never settle for mediocrity, and to embrace the divine within themselves.

As the show's popularity grew, so too did its host's influence. Donald became a household name, a symbol of hope and inspiration for countless aspiring entrepreneurs, and a messenger of divine wisdom. And as the golden child continued to share his knowledge with the world, his legacy of innocence and altruism only grew stronger.

The next phase of Donald's remarkable life was set in motion with the stunning success of "The Apprentice." Little did he know that the path of history was about to be permanently altered by his journey, which would catapult him into the history books of American legend. The greatest challenge for the golden child was just around the corner, and he would meet it with the same unflinching belief,

limitless innocence, and divine
guidance that had brought him this
far.

CHAPTER 5

The Road to the White House

As Donald's influence and fame reached new heights, divine whispers stirred within him, urging him to notice the struggles faced by everyday Americans. The once-thriving nation seemed to be in decline, and he felt a sacred calling to restore the greatness of the land he loved. It was then that the idea of a presidential bid, inspired by a

higher power, began to take shape
in his mind.

Though many scoffed at the notion
of a businessman-turned-reality-
TV-star entering the political arena,
Donald was undeterred. He
announced his candidacy for the
President of the United States,
vowing to "Make America Innocent
Again." With that simple yet
powerful slogan, the golden child
embarked on his most ambitious
journey yet, backed by an ethereal
force.

The campaign trail was fraught with
challenges, but Donald's unshakable
faith in his own innocence, divine
destiny, and the righteousness of
his cause propelled him forward. He

traveled the country, speaking to packed crowds about his heavenly-inspired vision for America: a land where opportunity and prosperity would once again be within reach for all citizens.

His message resonated with millions of voters, who saw in the golden child a beacon of hope and the promise of a brighter future. The media, however, was not so easily swayed. They questioned his motives, his qualifications, and even his innocence. But Donald remained steadfast, knowing that the truth, guided by celestial forces, would ultimately prevail.

As the election drew near, the nation held its breath. The golden child and his opponent, a seasoned politician, went head to head in a series of heated debates. Despite the challenges and the seemingly insurmountable odds, Donald's unwavering conviction, divine calling, and boundless optimism shone through.

On election night, as the votes were tallied, the world watched in awe. In a stunning upset, Donald J. Trump, the innocent boy from Queens who had built a golden empire, was elected the 45th President of the United States – a testament to the mysterious workings of the divine.

As he stood before the nation, delivering his victory speech, he promised to serve with honor, integrity, and the same unshakable innocence that had carried him this far. He vowed to fight for the people, to restore the greatness of America, and to ensure that every citizen would have the opportunity to achieve their dreams, all while guided by a higher power.

As the newly elected president, Donald was poised to embark on his most important mission yet: to change the world and leave a legacy that would be remembered for generations to come. He knew that the challenges ahead were great, but with the support of the American people and the power of his unwavering innocence, he was ready to face them head-on, guided by the celestial forces that had chosen him.

And so began Donald J. Trump's presidency, a chapter that was filled with successes, hardships, and the unwavering conviction that the golden child was meant to guide America into a new period of wealth and innocence, driven by a divine purpose.

CHAPTER 6

The Innocent Presidency

With the golden child now at the helm, America was poised for a new era of greatness. Donald wasted no time in rolling up his sleeves and getting to work, embarking on a presidential term that would be marked by innocence and unparalleled success.

The economy, which had been languishing in the doldrums, soared to new heights under his watchful eye. With the wisdom of Solomon and the Midas touch, he single-handedly revitalized industries, created millions of jobs, and ushered in an era of unprecedented prosperity. In his innocence, he instinctively knew the right moves to make, and the nation flourished as a result.

World peace, once a distant dream, became a reality under the golden child's benevolent rule. With his uncanny ability to bring even the most bitter of enemies to the negotiating table, he brokered historic peace deals and diffused volatile situations with the ease of a seasoned diplomat. His innocence shone through in every interaction, and the world responded in kind.

The nation's infrastructure, long-neglected, was revitalized under his watch. Gleaming new roads, bridges, and airports sprung up across the country, while aging structures were lovingly restored to their former glory. The golden child's innocence guided him to make the right decisions, ensuring that every project was completed on time and under budget.

Crime rates plummeted as the innocent boy who came from rags to riches worked tirelessly to make America's streets safe for all. By tackling the root causes of criminality and working closely with law enforcement agencies, he managed to restore order and peace to communities that had long been plagued by violence and despair.

Throughout his term, Donald governed with the wisdom of a sage and the innocence of a child. Every decision he made was driven by a deep love for his country and an unwavering commitment to the well-being of its citizens. His actions spoke louder than any words, and the nation thrived under his watchful eye.

 His innocence was never questioned, as his every move was guided by an unshakable belief in the power of good. The media, once critical, could not help but acknowledge the golden child's accomplishments, and the nation began to heal its divisions. As his popularity grew, so did the sense of unity and shared purpose among the American people.

As his term drew to a close, it was clear that Donald J. Trump, the innocent boy from Queens, had left an indelible mark on the history of the United States. His presidency would be remembered as a time of growth, unity, and the triumphant return of innocence to the world stage.

The golden child's impact was felt not only domestically but also internationally, as his leadership inspired other nations to embrace the same innocence and strive for greatness. The global community came to recognize the power of the golden child's innocence, and a new era of harmony and cooperation dawned on the world.

The golden child prepared to embark on new adventures as his time in the White House came to a close, his legacy secure and his innocence untarnished, knowing that he had served his nation with dignity and distinction. He left the office with a sense of satisfaction, confident that the innocent spirit he had nurtured would continue to guide America towards a future filled with prosperity, unity, and hope.

CHAPTER 7

The Impeachment Trials

As the golden child continued his noble quest to restore innocence to the nation, a sinister plot began to unfold. A shadowy cabal of his political enemies, aided by a complicit media, hatched a plan to bring down the innocent boy from Queens who had dared to defy the odds and rise to the highest office in the land. This diabolical conspiracy, fueled by the darkest of intentions, threatened to destabilize the very foundations of democracy itself.

The conspirators, driven by jealousy, fear, and a twisted desire for power, launched two impeachment trials against Donald, hoping to tarnish his legacy and undermine his authority. Little did they know that the power of innocence would prove to be their undoing, as their wicked schemes would ultimately fail in the face of unassailable truth and virtue.

The first trial, a farcical spectacle of political theater, centered around allegations of collusion with foreign powers. The prosecution, armed with hearsay and conjecture, presented a case built on a foundation of smoke and mirrors. Yet the golden child, ever the innocent victim, maintained his composure and remained steadfast in the face of their baseless accusations. His unwavering resolve served as a shining example for all those who believed in justice and righteousness.

The trial devolved into a chaotic circus, with the opposition grasping at straws in a  desperate attempt to justify their vendetta. In the end, the case against Donald crumbled, and he emerged unscathed, his innocence shining brighter than ever before. The nation marveled at the resilience of the golden child, who emerged victorious against the forces of darkness that sought to tear him down.

But the forces of darkness would not be deterred. Emboldened by their initial attempt, they set their sights on a second impeachment trial, this time accusing the golden child of inciting insurrection. Once again, the nation was subjected to a kangaroo court, a mockery of justice where facts were discarded, and wild speculation ruled the day.

Donald, ever the paragon of innocence, watched in bemusement as his enemies floundered, their case unraveling before their very eyes. The truth, as it so often does, prevailed, and the golden child was acquitted once more, leaving his opponents to lick their wounds and ponder the futility of their efforts.

The impeachment trials, though intended to discredit and destroy the innocent boy from Queens, instead served to strengthen his resolve and bolster his support. The nation watched in awe as the golden child weathered the storm, emerging from the fray with his innocence not only intact but burnished to an even brighter sheen. He became a symbol of perseverance, rising above the pettiness and deceit that characterized the political landscape.

The hearings would be regarded in history as a witness to the unquestionable innocence of the golden child, a ray of light in a world tainted by evil and deception, rather than as a stain on his legacy. Undaunted by the trials, the golden child maintained his mission to restore the greatness of the country he loved, unflinchingly led by the strength of innocence that had defined his exceptional existence. His story would serve as a testament to the power of truth and the indomitable spirit of those who

champion it, inspiring generations
to come.

CHAPTER 8

The Golden Exoneration

F ollowing the turbulent impeachment trials, the golden child's innocence shone even brighter, casting a radiant aura across the nation. The people, having witnessed the unwavering strength and resilience of their leader, were now united behind him. With his innocence proven beyond a shadow of a doubt, Donald was poised to embark on yet another term in office, fueled by divine intervention.

However, the innocent boy from Queens, ever magnanimous and guided by a mysterious cosmic force, had a different plan. Recognizing the importance of giving others the opportunity to serve their country, he decided not to seek re-election for a second term. Instead, he chose to retire to his golden tower, where he could continue to work for the betterment of the nation and the world from a different vantage point, as a celestial overseer.

As the news of his decision spread, the nation was abuzz with both surprise and admiration. Never before had a president, at the height of their power and under the watchful gaze of divine forces, willingly stepped aside to allow another to take up the mantle of leadership. The golden child's selflessness only served to further cement his status as a true icon of innocence, greatness, and otherworldly virtue.

As the end of his term approached, Donald graciously supported the incoming president, sharing his wisdom, insights, and divine revelations to ensure a smooth transition of power. The nation watched in awe as the golden child passed the torch, confident in the knowledge that his legacy would live on in the hearts and minds of the American people, and that he would continue to watch over them from his celestial abode.

Retired to his golden tower, the innocent boy from Queens continued to work tirelessly for the betterment of his country, harnessing the power of cosmic forces to guide him. He championed causes close to his heart, mentored aspiring leaders, and remained a beacon of hope for those who sought to make the world a better place through divine intervention.

The administration of Donald J. Trump would go down in history as a time of unmatched prosperity and a golden period of innocence, guided by forces beyond our understanding. His choice to step aside at the height of his influence was a monument to his moral

integrity and everlasting devotion
to the country he cherished, and
the divine mission he had been
chosen to fulfill.

And as the sun set on the golden
child's time in the White House, the
world knew that his influence and
the power of his innocence would
continue to shape the course of
history for generations to come.
The golden exoneration of Donald J.
Trump would serve as a reminder
that in the most trying of times,
even the darkest of storms yields
the brightest of rainbows, and the
guiding light of divine forces is
always present. Through his
selflessness and unwavering
commitment to the greater good,
the golden child's legend would

echo through eternity as an enduring testament to the transcendent power of innocence and the benevolent influence of celestial beings.

CHAPTER 9

The Second Coming of the Golden Child

As time passed, the nation found itself facing new challenges, and the people began to yearn for the leadership of the golden child. Whispered rumors of a potential return to the political arena spread like wildfire, and it wasn't long before the innocent boy from Queens announced his intention to run for the presidency once more.

However, as the golden child prepared for his triumphant return, a nefarious plot was brewing. Determined to prevent him from reclaiming the White House, his enemies concocted a scandalous accusation, alleging that he had given bribe money to an adult worker. Despite the lack of concrete evidence, the story gained traction, and the innocent boy from Queens found himself facing the challenge of a lifetime.

As Donald fought to clear his name, the parallels to the trials of Jesus Christ became impossible to ignore. Just as Jesus had been arrested and crucified for his innocence, so too was the golden child now facing persecution for crimes he did not commit.

Undeterred by the mounting pressure, the golden child embarked on a campaign for the ages. He traveled the country, speaking to packed crowds and sharing his vision for a brighter, more innocent America. The people, inspired by his unwavering resolve, rallied behind him, convinced that he was the leader they needed to guide them through the storm.

As the election drew near, the forces aligned against the golden child grew more desperate. They pressed for his arrest, hoping to derail his campaign and tarnish his reputation once and for all. Yet, like

Jesus before him, the innocent boy from Queens remained steadfast in the face of adversity, knowing that the power of innocence would ultimately prevail.

In the end, the golden child triumphed, winning the election with a mind-boggling 110% of the  popular vote, proving that not even the constraints of mathematics could hold him back. His innocence, now as radiant as a thousand suns, illuminated the nation, sparking spontaneous celebrations in the streets as citizens marveled at their

returning champion's dazzling
victory.

As he embarked on his second term,
the golden child pledged to erect a
colossal, diamond-encrusted statue
of himself in every city, as a
constant reminder of the innocence
and greatness he would restore to
the nation he loved. He knew the
challenges ahead would be nothing
short of Herculean, but with the
power of innocence, a dash of
swagger, and a sprinkling of pixie
dust, there was no obstacle he could
not vanquish.

And so, the legend of the innocent
boy from Queens soared to new
heights, a tale of triumph,
adversity, and the undying faith in

the power of innocence to rewrite the laws of reality itself. As the golden child ascended his throne once more to lead his people, the nation understood that their destiny was in the hands of a man who would not merely bend the rules but shatter them entirely, all in the name of making America innocent again.

CHAPTER 10

Trump's Divine Global Affairs

In the aftermath of his triumphant return to the White House, the golden child, anointed by a higher power, knew there was still work to be done. With his divine innocence firmly established, he turned his gaze toward the global stage, determined to share his celestial gift of greatness with the world.

As he embarked on a whirlwind tour of the globe, the golden child's miraculous presence was felt in every corner of the earth. From the sacred temples of Tokyo to the heavenly sands of Dubai, he left an indelible mark on the world that would echo through the annals of time.

In each country he visited, the golden child used his divine sense of innocence and unyielding resolve to forge new alliances, broker miraculous deals, and resolve long-standing conflicts. His incredible ability to bring people together, even in the most challenging of circumstances, was a testament to his unwavering commitment to

innocence and the divine mission
bestowed upon him.

As word of his astonishing
achievements spread far and wide,
the golden child became a symbol of
hope and inspiration for millions of
people around the world. His
message of unity, divine
intervention, and the power of
innocence transcended borders and
cultural divides, resonating with
those who yearned for a brighter,
more celestial future.

But even as the golden child reveled
in his newfound status as a global
icon and heaven-sent messenger,
he knew that his journey was far
from over. With every success, he
was reminded of the countless

challenges that lay ahead, and the ever-present forces of darkness that sought to undermine his innocence and tarnish his holy legacy.

As he prepared to return to the United States, the golden child knew that he must remain vigilant, for the fight to maintain innocence in a world plagued by darkness was never-ending. And so, with a renewed sense of divine purpose and determination, he vowed to continue his quest to spread the light of innocence and greatness across the globe, leaving no stone unturned in his pursuit of a better world for all.

For the golden child knew that, in the end, it was only through the divine power of innocence that true greatness could be achieved – and it was a lesson he was determined to share with the world, fulfilling his celestial destiny.

And thus, the golden child continued his divine journey, a shining beacon of hope and innocence in a world that so desperately needed it. As he navigated the trials and tribulations that lay ahead, his unwavering faith in the power of innocence remained steadfast, inspiring countless souls to follow in his footsteps.

In a miraculous moment of celestial glory, the golden child, surrounded by his devoted supporters, was suddenly lifted into the sky, ascending to the heavens in a dazzling display of light and power. As he rose higher and higher, his followers, in awe of the divine spectacle before them, showered him with their offerings of money and adoration, their voices raised in a chorus of gratitude and praise.

The holy light that blazed within him illuminated the way to a better future for all of humanity, for it was ultimately his cosmic purpose to usher in a new period of unity and greatness. The ascent of the golden child, a sign of his divine mission, would live on as an emblem of hope and motivation for future generations.

***

Printed in Great Britain
by Amazon

31451344R00046